For
Laura
&

1988

SUNDAY

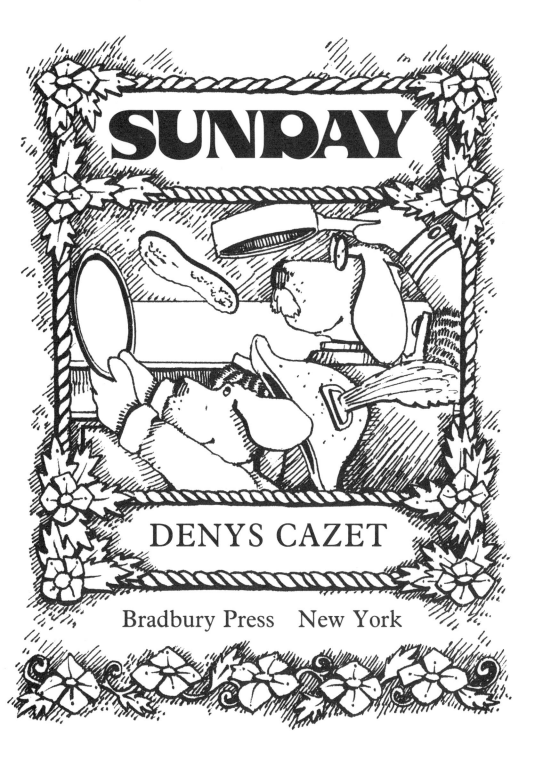

DENYS CAZET

Bradbury Press   New York

For Csaba, Dawn, Alexandra,
Jake, and Dominic too!

CONTENTS

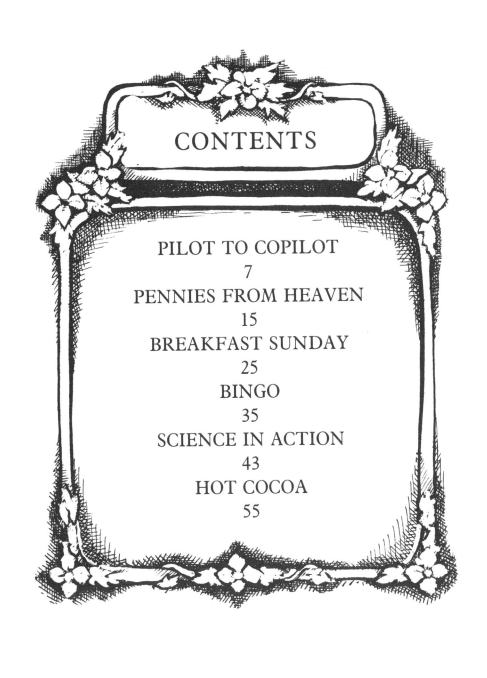

PILOT TO COPILOT

Barney sat up in bed.

"Hang on, Grandma!" he shouted. "We're coming to save you!"

"Thank heavens!" Grandma whispered, sitting on the edge of the bed.

Barney rubbed his eyes and yawned. "I was dreaming," he said.

"Time to wake up," said Grandma. "Time to get ready for church."

Barney slid out of bed and put on his clothes.

"I was dreaming that King Kong carried you away to be Queen Kong."

"Mercy sakes," said Grandma. "Tie your shoes."

Barney tied his shoes. "Grandpa and me were riding a rocket-bicycle. I was the pilot and Grandpa was the copilot. We were going so fast the bicycle was whistling."

"That was the tea kettle," said Grandma, walking back into the kitchen.

"You punched King Kong in the nose!" said Barney. "Boy, was he mad!"

Grandma poured the hot water into the teapot. She pointed at Grandpa's bedroom door.

"Go wake up Grandpa and remind him to put on his uniform. Today is Breakfast Sunday. The Knights of the Three Pillars are going to be cooking breakfast."

"Roger, wilco," said Barney.

"And *don't* remind him that we're playing Bingo at the Piggermans' this afternoon," said Grandma, pouring herself a cup of tea.

"Double roger, wilco, over and out," said Barney.

He peeked into Grandpa's bedroom. Grandpa was snoring.

Barney leaned across Grandpa's bed. He whispered into his ear. "Pilot to co-pilot. Pilot to copilot. Time to get up and go to church."

Grandpa snored louder.

"Pilot to copilot. Pilot to copilot," Barney repeated. "Time to get up and go to church."

Grandpa snored so loud the windows rattled.

Barney lifted Grandpa's ear. "Pilot to copilot. Pilot to copilot. Time to get up and put on your uniform. You have to cook breakfast after church. This is a message from your captain."

Grandpa snored so loud that a picture fell off the wall.

Barney lifted both of Grandpa's ears. "Pilot to copilot. Pilot to copilot. This is a message from your captain . . . Captain Grandma!"

Grandpa's eyes popped open.

"Copilot to pilot. Copilot to pilot," said Grandpa. "I read you loud and clear!"

"Roger, copilot!" said Barney. "Over and out!"

PENNIES FROM HEAVEN

The church was crowded.

"I knew we were going to be late," whispered Grandma.

They sat down between the Zebramans and the Piggermans.

Grandpa's medals clanked.

"Shhh," said Mrs. Zebraman.

Harold Piggerman turned around and whispered to Barney, "How come you're late?"

"Grandpa's snorer got stuck," Barney whispered.

"Those are double-wow medals," whispered Harold. "What a great sword!"

Barney leaned forward. "My Grandpa's president of the Nights of the Three Pillows," he said proudly.

"Pillars," whispered Grandpa, adjusting his sword.

The sword poked Mr. Piggerman.

"Ouch!" he cried.

"Shhh," said Mrs. Zebraman, "I'm trying to hear the sermon."

The sermon went on for a long time.

Barney's stomach grumbled.

"Was that you or me?" Grandpa whispered.

"Me," whispered Barney, covering his stomach with his cap.

Grandpa's stomach rumbled.

"That was you," Barney whispered, leaning against Grandma.

"You must be hungry," said Grandma. Barney nodded.

Grandma handed Barney twenty-five cents. "Here comes Mr. Rhinotino with the collection basket."

Barney's stomach rumbled.

Grandpa's stomach rumbled.

Suddenly, both their stomachs rumbled at the same time.

Harold looked at his father. "I think it's going to rain," he whispered.

"Shhh," said Mrs. Zebraman.

Mrs. Piggerman handed Harold a dollar. She pointed at Mr. Rhinotino, the banker.

Mr. Rhinotino held a long-handled basket in front of the Piggermans.

Harold dropped in his dollar.

Mr. Piggerman held up a twenty-dollar bill, snapped it once, and then let it fall into the basket.

Mr. Rhinotino nodded and smiled.

Grandma slipped in a five-dollar bill and Barney dropped in his twenty-five cents.

Grandpa reached into the basket and took out three dollars.

Mr. Rhinotino cleared his throat loudly and shook his head.

"What are you doing?" whispered Grandma.

Grandpa shrugged. "Getting change!"

Grandma raised both her eyebrows.

Grandpa put the money back.

Mr. Rhinotino pulled on the basket. It wouldn't budge.

"What's the matter, Grandpa?" Barney asked.

"One of my medals is stuck to the basket," Grandpa whispered.

Mr. Rhinotino cleared his throat again. "Will you please let go!"

"Just a minute," whispered Grandpa.

Barney tugged on the medal.

Mr. Rhinotino tugged on the basket.

"Let go of my medal!" said Grandpa, pulling on the basket.

"Let go of my money!" shouted Mr. Rhinotino. He jerked on the basket so hard that Grandpa's medal popped off and fell in Barney's lap.

The basket twisted backward and
sailed over Grandma's head.

"Mercy sakes!" cried Grandma.

"Good Lord!" cried the minister.

Coins bounced down the aisles and
paper money floated down from the
ceiling.

The organist watched a twenty-dollar bill float down from the rafters and settle gently on her lap.

She played "Pennies from Heaven."

While the choir sang, Barney pinned Grandpa's medal back on his coat.

"Thank you," whispered Grandpa.

"You're welcome," whispered Barney.

"Shhh!" said Mrs. Zebraman.

BREAKFAST SUNDAY

"Everybody ready?" Grandpa asked, looking around the big kitchen.

"Everybody except the waiters," said Mr. Rabbitski.

"Who's in charge of the waiters?"

"Enrico Rhinotino," said Dr. Storkmeyer.

25

"Well . . . where is he?"

"Still picking up the money that flew out of the collection basket," said Mr. Rabbitski.

"Oh," said Grandpa.

"What are we going to do?" asked Dr. Storkmeyer. "We can't work in here and wait on tables at the same time."

The doors to the dining hall swung open. The crowd swarmed across the room like ants at a picnic.

Barney waved as he walked by with three of his friends.

"That's it!" said Grandpa, pointing at Barney. "You are now my number one head waiter. And you, Louie Rabbitski, and you, Emily Rabbitski, and yes, you too, Harold Piggerman, are all generals, first class."

"What do you mean?" asked Harold.

"He means," said Emily, "that we're in charge of serving breakfast."

"Let's go!" said Barney.

Grandpa slapped a stack of pancakes on Harold's serving platter. "Now we're rolling!" he shouted.

Barney ran up to the counter. "Mrs. Holstein wants to know if the milk is fresh."

"Fresh squeezed this morning," said Grandpa.

"More pancakes," puffed Harold. "More pancakes!"

Mr. Rabbitski flipped six pancakes onto Harold's platter.

"Grandpa," said Louie.

"What?" said Grandpa Spanielson.

"My Grandpa," said Louie. "Grandpa Rabbitski."

Mr. Rabbitski looked over the counter at Louie. "Yes, my favorite grandson?"

"Grandma wants to know if you made the French toast with turtle eggs again."

"You made the French toast with turtle eggs?" said Grandpa Spanielson.

"Last month," said Grandpa Rabbitski. "They were half price!"

"Tell your Grandma these eggs come from Mrs. Poulet's Coop-Op on East 12th," said Grandpa Spanielson.

"Right," said Louie.

"Pancakes," puffed Harold. "More pancakes!"

Mr. Rabbitski flipped eight pancakes onto Harold's platter.

"Someone's eating a lot of pancakes," said Grandpa Spanielson.

"The Piggermans," said Emily.

"We're a big family," protested Harold.

"You're not supposed to serve one and eat two!" said Emily.

"I have to fuel the furnace," said Harold, running back to the tables.

"More pancakes for the furnace!" said Mr. Rabbitski, and he flipped ten pancakes into the air at the same time.

"Triple wow!" said Barney. "Do you

think you can do that, Grandpa?"

Grandpa Rabbitski smiled and handed Grandpa Spanielson the spatula.

"Easy. Watch this!" Grandpa Spanielson flipped twelve pancakes into the air at the same time.

They stuck to the ceiling.

"Oh, Mr. Spanielson," called Mrs. Piggerman, walking up to the counter. "We seem to be out of pancakes."

She shoved the empty platter toward Mr. Rabbitski. "Hurry," she said.

Mrs. Piggerman looked down at Barney and smiled.

The pancakes peeled off the ceiling and fell onto the platter with twelve loud plops!

Mrs. Piggerman looked back at the platter. "Ahhh," she said, walking away, "that's more like it!"

Grandpa looked at Barney.

"Fuel for the furnace," he said.

BINGO

Barney stopped in front of the Piggermans' house.

"Our house is next door," said Grandpa. "Why are we stopping at the Piggermans'?"

"Bingo," said Barney.

"Bingo!" moaned Grandpa. "I forgot. Today is Grandma's Bingo day."

Barney tugged on Grandpa's arm. "Come on, Grandpa. We'll be a team."

"I don't know why Grandma won't let us be a team on poker night," muttered Grandpa.

"There's Grandma," said Barney. "Sitting next to Mrs. Rabbitski."

"Hi, Grandma. Hi, Mrs. Rabbitski," said Barney, sitting down.

Grandma gave Barney a hug. "You did a wonderful job at breakfast."

"And you did too, Mr. Spanielson," said Mrs. Rabbitski. "Thank you for not letting Mr. Rabbitski make the French toast."

"Mr. Rabbitski's still washing the dishes," said Barney.

"Now I know why he volunteered," Grandpa muttered.

"So far, I've won nine dollars!" said Grandma.

"Nine dollars!" said Grandpa, sitting down. "Give this team a card!"

Grandma took one of her washable Bingo cards out of her purse and handed it to Barney. "And here," she said. "Use my markers."

Grandma poured some dried lima beans into a little dish.

Barney marked the free space.

"*Bingo!*" Grandpa shouted.

Mrs. Zebraman gasped. "I haven't even called out the first number yet, Mr. Spanielson. How can you have Bingo already?"

"Right here," said Grandpa. "See! Right in the middle."

Grandma and Mrs. Rabbitski sighed.

"You have to have five in a row, Grandpa," said Barney.

"Right," said Grandpa. "Cancel that Bingo."

Mrs. Zebraman nodded at Grandpa. "Are you ready, Mr. Spanielson?"

Grandpa looked at Barney. "Ready?"

"Ready," said Barney.

Mrs. Zebraman called out several more numbers.

"We're doing pretty good, Grandpa," said Barney. "See. We only need this to win."

Grandpa looked at the card.

"I-21," called Mrs. Zebraman.

"*Bingo!*" Grandpa shouted. "We won!"

"Grandpa," whispered Barney, "we don't have 21."

"Suffering stinkweed," said Grandpa. "Must be these new trifocals!"

Grandma waved to Mrs. Zebraman to continue calling the numbers.

"I give up," said Grandpa.

"Quitters never win," Grandma warned.

"I-23," called Mrs. Zebraman.

"*Bingo!*" Barney shouted. "We won, Grandpa!"

"I knew it!" shouted Grandpa.

"I thought you quit," said Grandma.

"Just resting," said Grandpa.

Mrs. Zebraman handed Barney three dollars.

"Here, Grandma," said Barney. "This dollar is for you."

"Thank you," said Grandma.

"And Grandpa and I each get a dollar," said Barney, "because we're a team."

"Bingo!" said Grandpa.

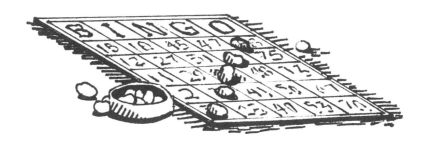

SCIENCE IN ACTION

Grandpa and Barney sat on the Pig-germans' back porch enjoying the late afternoon sun.

"Oh, dear," said Mr. Piggerman, sitting down. "Oh, dear, oh, dear!"

"What's the matter?"

Harold held up a wet sock. "The clothes dryer is broken," he said, "and Mom is mad at Pop 'cause he can't fix it!"

"My Grandpa can fix it," said Barney. "He fixed it so that all the lights in the house went out at the same time. He fixed my science project . . ."

"And he fixed Mrs. Spanielson's vacuum cleaner so good it sucked up a pair of Barney's pants and his goldfish," Harold said.

"Now, now boys," said Grandpa, "I'm sure Mr. Piggerman . . ."

"Oh, please, Mr. Spanielson," Mr. Piggerman pleaded, "take a look at it."

"Oh, all right," said Grandpa. "I guess

it won't hurt to take a little peek."

They went into the laundry room.

Grandpa and Barney peeked behind the dryer. "Hmmm," said Grandpa.

"Hmmm," said Barney.

"Wrench," said Grandpa.

"Wrench," said Barney, handing Grandpa the wrench.

"Golf club," said Grandpa.

"Golf club," said Barney, handing Grandpa the golf club.

Grandpa held up his hand.

"Stand back," said Barney.

Mr. Piggerman and Harold moved to the other side of the room.

Grandpa gave the machine a loud whack with the golf club. "There," he said. "Now try it!"

Barney threw the wet clothes into the machine and closed the round door.

Harold turned the dial. The machine hummed and whirred softly.

"See," said Harold. "Mr. Spanielson and Barney can fix anything."

The machine hummed louder.

It began to rock back and forth.

"Why is it doing that?" Mr. Piggerman asked. "It didn't used to do that!"

"Science," said Grandpa. "It must be going through the unknown cycle."

The machine rumbled and coughed and began to hop up and down.

Mr. Piggerman hid behind the hot water heater.

The machine hopped and rocked and rolled and jumped and made swirly, whirly sounds that went faster and faster and faster until, all of a sudden, it stopped with a loud *swoop*!

The door swung open and Harold and Barney looked in.

"Gone!" said Harold.

"What do you mean gone?" asked Mr. Piggerman.

"Gone," said Barney. "There isn't anything in there."

"Oh, merciful gravy," said Mr. Piggerman, sitting on the floor.

"Science in action," said Grandpa, opening up the back door. "The amount of Newtonian-Flux exceeded the velocity of the Whatsinfratz."

"What's that mean?" Barney asked.

"It means, I think Mrs. Piggerman's corset went up the vent pipe!"

Barney and Harold followed Grandpa into the backyard.

Grandpa looked up. "Suffering stinkweed!" he shouted.

Mrs. Piggerman's underwear hung from the television antenna.

"Wait until my mother sees this," said Harold. "You'll be able to hear her scream all the way around the block!"

"Here comes Grandma," said Barney.

"Ready to go home and have a little soup?" Grandma asked.

Grandpa nodded.

Barney waved good-bye to Harold, but Harold didn't notice.

Barney raced ahead. He ran up the back steps and then waited for Grandpa and Grandma to catch up.

When they reached the top of the
steps, Grandma stopped and sighed.

"Isn't the setting sun lovely," she said.
"It's so quiet, the whole world seems
to be at peace."

"EEEEEEEEEEEEEEEKKK!"
screamed Mrs. Piggerman.

HOT COCOA

Grandma put the empty soup bowls in the kitchen sink and looked out the window.

"Mercy sakes alive!" she cried.

Barney dropped the dish towel. "What's the matter, Grandma?"

"Look!" she said. "Mrs. Piggerman is drying her clothes on the T.V. antenna!"

Grandpa put down his newspaper. "There's a lot of good air up there buzzing around with nothing to do," he said. "Might as well use it!"

Grandma raised her left eyebrow.

"How do you wear that thing hanging up there, Grandma?" Barney asked.

"Never mind," Grandma said.

"I've seen them in catalogs," said Barney.

"Time to brush your teeth," said Grandma. "Go on!"

"It's giant!" said Barney, running into the bathroom.

Grandpa looked out the window. "By gollies, he's right!"

Grandma raised her right eyebrow and closed the curtains. "Mind your own business!" she said.

Barney ran into his bedroom and jumped into bed. He straightened up his comic books. "Ready!" he shouted.

Grandpa and Grandma walked into Barney's room.

"Got any stories about bicycles and King Kong, Grandpa?" Barney asked. "I had a dream last night about chasing King Kong on a bicycle."

Grandma smiled and sat down on the bed. "Tell Barney the story about how you took me for a bicycle ride, and then how King Kong took you for one!"

"By gollies, I wish you'd forget that one," Grandpa grumbled.

"How about The Three Bears?" said Grandpa.

"King Kong and the bicycles," said Barney.

"I'll tell you what," said Grandma. "I'll tell the story and Grandpa can make the cocoa."

"Double wow," said Barney, fluffing up his pillow.

"Once upon a time," said Grandma, "before the days of Barney, when Grandpa was much younger, but not nearly as handsome, he took me on a bicycle ride.

"Well, feeling young and frisky, he raced ahead of me. Of course, I raced ahead of him, and soon we were both racing down the road when . . ."

Grandma stopped. "Go on, go on," she said to Grandpa. "Go make the cocoa."

"Hummph," muttered Grandpa, walking into the kitchen. He took out a small pan and put it on the stove.

He mixed the cocoa with the milk and stirred it.

He took three cocoa mugs off the shelf, poured in the hot cocoa, and set the steaming mugs on a tray.

Grandpa closed the back door and hung up a clean apron for Grandma.

He picked up the tray and brought it into Barney's bedroom.

Barney and Grandma were asleep.

Grandpa set the tray on the dresser and sat down quietly.

He held the warm mug between his paws and watched them sleeping.

He thought about the day. He thought about Sundays past and about all the days before Barney.

He thought about Grandma and the bicycle race and what it was like when they were young.

And then, he thought about now, that very moment.

Grandpa sipped his cocoa slowly and smiled.